THE BIG GREEN HELP™

DORA EXPLORER®

Dora Celebrates Earth Day!

by Emily Sollinger   illustrated by Dave Aikins

Simon Spotlight/Nickelodeon
New York   London   Toronto   Sydney

Based on the TV series *Dora the Explorer*® as seen on Nickelodeon®

SIMON SPOTLIGHT
An imprint of Simon & Schuster Children's Publishing Division
1230 Avenue of the Americas, New York, New York 10020

First Edition
2 4 6 8 10 9 7 5 3 1
ISBN-13: 978-1-4169-7580-9
ISBN-10: 1-4169-7580-2

¡Hola! I'm Dora! Today is Earth Day, and we're having a party at Play Park to celebrate. Do you know what Earth Day is?

Earth Day is when we celebrate the Earth and learn about ways to take care of it. There are things we can do every day to help protect the Earth.

I have an idea! I'm going to ask all of my friends and family what they do to help save the Earth. I'll put all of their tips in an Earth Day scrapbook that I can bring to the party to share with everyone.

My best friend, Boots, says he always makes sure not to waste water. He takes short showers and turns off the faucet when he's brushing his teeth. Can you think of any other ways to save water?

Here's an Earth Day idea! If you have water left in your drinking glass, you can use it to water your house plants. Do you see any plants that need watering?

WAYS TO SAVE WATER!
1. _____
2. _____
3. _____

My *mami* says it's important to turn off the lights when we aren't using them. We can save a lot of energy this way. We can also turn out the lights during the day when there is plenty of sunlight. How else can we save energy?

My cousin Diego knows a great way to save energy. He always rides his bike to school instead of riding in a car. You can also walk, roller-skate, skip, or run! Diego says these are great ways to spend time outdoors and get exercise while keeping the air clean. Sometimes he even finds animals to rescue along the way!

My Bike

SAVE ENERGY

My *papi* loves to cook. When he goes to the supermarket to buy groceries, he brings his own cloth bags with him. He reuses the same bags every time he goes shopping.

REUSE

Reuse!

When *Papi* makes my lunch, he puts it in a special bag. We wash the bag, and I use it again!

My *abuela* is careful about saving energy too. When she's cooking or preparing food, she always decides what she wants to get before opening the refrigerator door. If you leave the door open for a long time, you'll let out cold air and the refrigerator will use more energy to keep working.

Even my baby brother and sister can help save the Earth. When the twins outgrow their toys and books, we won't throw them away. Instead, we'll pass them along to other babies who can use them.

DONATIONS

SHARE

My friend Isa loves to plant fruits, vegetables, trees, and flowers in her garden. Growing flowers, trees, and other plants helps make the air we breathe clean and fresh. It's a great thing to do on Earth Day . . . and every day!

My friend Benny saves energy by playing outside whenever he can. There are so many games we can play outside. I love soccer! What's your favorite outdoor game?

LET'S PLAY!!!

Power Off!

Turn OFF!

SHUT DOWN!

My friend Tico always makes sure to recycle properly. He separates cans, bottles, and paper from regular trash and places them in special containers. The cans, bottles, and paper can be recycled and used to make other things—like books and toys! I see some things that need to be recycled. Do you see them? Where?

THE DAILY PAPER
DORA RECYCLES!

THE DAILY PAPER

RECYCLE

I'm so glad that all of my friends and family work so hard to help take care of the Earth. I learned a lot from them. Did you?

Now it's time to go to the Earth Day party in Play Park. Oh, no! It looks like there's trash along the path. Will you help me pick it up?

Hooray! We cleared the path to the park. Thanks so much for helping. Now I'm going to share my Earth Day scrapbook with everyone at the party!

Every day can be Earth Day as long as we all pitch in!